Arthur Starter Book 01

ARTHUR

and the Big Sno

by Marc Brown

Long tail Books

“Look at all that snow!” said Arthur. “No school today.”

"Everyone's going to meet at the big hill," said Arthur.
Dad shook his head. "D.W.'s too small to walk in this deep snow. We have to wait for them to plow."

"Dad says we have to wait for the plow," said Arthur.
"We do," said Mom. "The big hill is too far for D.W. to walk."

Arthur sighed. "Well, then, I guess I'll go outside and play in the snow."
"Me too!" said D.W. "Help me get dressed."

Arthur helped D.W. put on her snowsuit.
“Pull!” said D.W.
Arthur pulled.

"Push!" said D.W.
Arthur pushed.

Outside, Arthur started to make a snowman.
D.W. just stood there.
“I can’t move in all this snow!” she said. “I want to go back in.”
“But we just got out here,” said Arthur.
“NOW!” said D.W.

“Let’s play Tower of Cows,” said D.W.
“But I want to go back outside,” said Arthur.
“Just one game,” said D.W.
“I’ll even let you go first.”

When the game was over, Arthur stood up to go back outside.

"Don't go yet," said D.W. "Read to me."

"But the snow . . . ," said Arthur.

"Just one story," said D.W. "Any one you want."

Arthur sighed. "Okay, but just one."

FROGGIE
2
BIG BOOK OF COLOR

Finally, the plow roared by.
"Yay!" Arthur shouted. "Now we can go!"
Then the phone rang.

TUCKER
ELIZA
MR. BUNNY

It was Francine.

"Hi, Arthur. The sledding was great!
You should have been there.
Oops, I have to go. The hot chocolate is ready. Bye."

“Are you ready, Arthur?” asked Dad.
“It’s too late,” he said. “I missed the sledding.
I missed the hot chocolate. I missed everything.”

“Oh, that’s too bad,” said Dad.
“I thought you might like to try out this new sled.”
“Wow!” shouted Arthur. “Let’s go!”

The new sled was really fast.
"We have the whole hill to ourselves!" said Arthur.

"Sometimes," said Mom, "good things are worth waiting for."